JACQUELINE PEARCE

Flood Warning

ILLUSTRATIONS BY Leanne Franson

ORCA BOOK PUBLISHERS

Library and Archives Canada Cataloguing in Publication

Pearce, Jacqueline, 1962-
Flood warning / Jacqueline Pearce ; illustrations by Leanne Franson.
(Orca echoes)

Issued also in electronic format.
ISBN 978-1-4598-0068-7

1. Floods--British Columbia--Fraser River Valley--Juvenile fiction.
2. Fraser River Valley (B.C.)--History--Juvenile fiction.   I. Franson,
PS8581.E26F56 2012   JC813'.6   C2011-907778-7

First published in the United States, 2012
Library of Congress Control Number: 2011943722

Summary: The Fraser River is about to flood, so Tom must get his family's dairy cows to safety
before it's too late. A historical story set in 1948, near the farming community of Agassiz.

Orca Book Publishers gratefully acknowledges the support for its publishing programs
provided by the following agencies: the Government of Canada through the Canada Book
Fund and the Canada Council for the Arts, and the Province of British Columbia
through the BC Arts Council and the Book Publishing Tax Credit.

MIX
Paper from
responsible sources
FSC
www.fsc.org   **FSC® C004071**

ANCIENT FOREST™
FRIENDLY

*Orca Book Publishers is dedicated to preserving the environment and has printed this book
on paper certified by the Forest Stewardship Council®.*

Cover artwork and interior illustrations by Leanne Franson
Author photo by Danielle Naherniak

ORCA BOOK PUBLISHERS
PO Box 5626, Stn. B
Victoria, BC Canada
V8R 6S4

ORCA BOOK PUBLISHERS
PO Box 468
Custer, WA USA
98240-0468

www.orcabook.com
Printed and bound in Canada.

15 14 13 12 • 4 3 2 1

Thanks go to my dad, Jack Pearce, and my father-in-law,
Bill Naherniak (also known as Farmer Bill*),*
who helped with the details of the farm and time period.
I would also like to thank the Agassiz-Harrison Museum
and the Chilliwack Museum and Archives.

—JP

To all those brave Canadians across this country who
courageously deal with floods and their aftermath.

—LF

CHAPTER ONE

The River

"Hi-ho, Silver! Away!" shouted Tom.

He was pretending to be the Lone Ranger, his favorite radio hero. Amos, Tom's scruffy black and brown dog, pricked up his ears. Amos seemed to know he was playing the part of Silver, the Lone Ranger's horse. Boy and dog took off running across the field.

*Dunt-da-dalunt-da-daluntuntun, dunt-da-dalunt-da-daluntuntun...*The show's opening music played in Tom's mind. Every Sunday evening, Tom and his parents gathered around the big radio in the living room. They listened to the adventures of the Lone Ranger, his fiery horse, Silver, and his faithful companion, Tonto. Every week, the heroic masked rider and his daring friend fought for law and order in the Old West.

"Wait up!" called Tom's friend, Peggy. She ran after Tom and Amos. Her two brown braids flew out behind her.

Ah, my faithful friend, Tonto, Tom thought as Peggy caught up to him. But he didn't say it out loud. Peggy always wanted to be the Lone Ranger, not the sidekick.

Amos barked loudly. Several brown and white cows trotted out of their way. Tom lifted his face to the warm sun. It was perfect weather for the May long weekend. He wished tomorrow was a holiday too.

They reached the wooden fence at the end of the field. Tom and Peggy stopped to catch their breath. Tom lifted a loose board at the bottom of the fence, so Amos could pass under. Then he and Peggy climbed over. They faced a tangle of low bushes and weedy alder trees.

"Come on!" said Tom. He waved a hand for Peggy to follow him. "We're almost at the river."

"Okay," Peggy said. "But this time I'll lead the way."

She pushed past Tom and ran down a trail through the underbrush. They could hear the sound of the river ahead. Peggy emerged from the trees and stopped in surprise. Tom and Amos almost bumped into her.

Usually, there was a wide gravel bank between the trees and the river. But now, the water had crept up over the rocks. It was lapping at a row of sandbags piled at the edge of the trees.

"Do you think it's going to flood?" Peggy asked.

"Nah," Tom said. "If the water gets any higher, the sandbags will stop it."

Each spring, when the snow melted in the mountains, the waters of the Fraser River rose. Two years ago, soldiers back from the Second World War had piled sandbags along the river. The sandbags acted like a dyke, or a low wall, to help keep the water from flooding the farmland.

3

"I don't know," Peggy said. She pointed to a spot where a section of sandbags had fallen over and left a gap. "Those sandbags don't look like they could stop much."

She glanced up at the sun, which was getting lower in the sky.

"I've got to get home to help with milking," she said.

"Me too," said Tom. There was never a holiday from milking.

Reluctantly, Tom turned away from the widening brown river. If there were a flood, what would the Lone Ranger do?

CHAPTER TWO

Milking Time

When they got back to Tom's house, the cows were already shuffling into the barn for milking. Peggy said goodbye and raced down the driveway. Her family's dairy farm was just across the road.

Tom forgot about the river and hurried into the barn. His dad was using a pitchfork to toss hay into the cows' feed troughs.

"You're late," Dad said, not looking up. He handed Tom the pitchfork. It was Tom's job to feed the cows. Tom's mom and dad did the milking.

Tom stuck the fork into a hay bale. He pulled out some loose hay and dropped it into the next stall. He finished putting out the hay and made sure the

cows were settled into their stalls. Then he went to help with the milking.

Dad was bent under a large brown and white cow. He directed streams of milk into a metal pail. When the pail was full, he passed it to Tom. It took all of Tom's strength to lift the pail. He dumped the milk into the tall metal container used for storing and shipping milk.

The family's dairy farm was small. They had ten Guernsey cows and some spring calves. The male calves had already been sold. Three female calves remained with their mothers. The adult cows had to be milked twice a day, early in the morning and before supper. Tom's parents did all the milking by hand. It took about an hour and a half to finish. When they bought a milking machine, it would be quicker.

It wasn't until the family was sitting around the kitchen table eating supper that Tom remembered the river.

"I went down to the river today with Amos and Peggy," Tom told his parents.

"So that's why you were late," said Dad, sounding annoyed. But his mouth quirked sideways. Tom knew he wasn't really mad.

"The river's getting pretty high," Tom said.

Tom's mom looked at her husband with concern. "It won't rise high enough to flood, will it?" she asked.

"I don't think there's anything to worry about," said Dad. But the smile had left his lips.

CHAPTER THREE

Alarm Call

Tom woke in the middle of the night. Someone was banging on the front door of the house. Amos got up from the floor beside Tom's bed. He barked twice, then padded out of the room and down the stairs.

Tom's parents stirred in the next bedroom. Dad's footsteps followed Amos down the stairs. The front door clicked opened. Tom could hear muffled voices, quiet but urgent. What was going on?

Tom climbed out of bed and listened at the top of the stairs. He heard the words *river* and *rising steadily*. A chill ran up his back.

"What are you doing up?" said his mother.

Tom turned to see Mom standing in the hallway. She had her housecoat on over her nightgown.

"Go back to bed," she said. "It's a school night."

"But I want to know what's happening," Tom said.

Dad appeared at the bottom of the stairs. "There's a flood warning all along the river!" he called up to them. "I'm going to help build up the sandbags."

"I want to help too," Tom said.

Mom put a hand on Tom's arm, holding him back. "It's nothing for you to worry about," she said. "The men will take care of it."

"I'm old enough to help," Tom said. But Mom did not give in.

She nudged him toward his bedroom. "There's school in the morning," she said. "You need to get your sleep."

Tom climbed back into bed. He heard the sound of the front door closing and men's voices outside the house. He checked to see his mom wasn't still in

the doorway. Then Tom jumped out of bed and hurried to the window.

A pickup truck was parked in the driveway below. It rumbled loudly. It was dark outside, but Tom could tell it was Peggy's dad's 1929 Ford. The light at the side of the house shone on her two older brothers in the back of the truck. Dad climbed into the cab next to Peggy's dad. The truck doors slammed shut, and the motor coughed into gear.

Tom leaned on the window ledge as the truck pulled away. He wished he was going with them. The Lone Ranger wouldn't stay home and do nothing.

CHAPTER FOUR

Rising Concern

The next morning, Dad was home in time for the milking.

"How's the river look?" Tom asked.

Dad shook his head. There were dark shadows under his eyes. "Still rising," he said. "Men are working steady, building up dykes. I've got to get back there as soon as I'm finished here."

"Can I come with you this time?" Tom asked.

Dad shook his head. "You've got school, and you're going to have to help around here when you get home. Now, hurry up with that hay," he said, striding into the barn. "We've got to finish quickly."

14

After the milking, Mom packed Dad some food and a thermos of coffee. He drove off with another group of men. Tom watched him go as he waited outside for Peggy. She and Tom walked to school together every morning.

"I wish I could go with my dad instead of going to school," Tom said when Peggy joined him.

"Me too," Peggy said.

Amos barked as if in agreement. He trotted in front of Tom and Peggy, leading the way to the shortcut across the back field and through the neighboring farms. The cows were now out grazing. The new calves stood close to their mothers.

"I wonder how high the river is," said Tom. He pictured the sagging row of sandbags they had seen yesterday. Was water pouring over the top and through the cracks? Had the men fixed the wall and made it higher?

When they reached the edge of the pasture, Tom and Peggy climbed the fence. Amos sat watching them. This was as far as he was allowed to go. He raised one brown eyebrow as if to say, *Are you sure I can't come with you?*

"Sorry, boy," Tom said. He knew how Amos felt. He hated being left behind when his dad was off doing something important.

"Hey," Peggy said, breaking through Tom's thoughts. "This field is soggy."

Tom felt mud tug at his shoes. When he lifted one foot, water slowly filled his footprint.

"That's strange," Tom said. "Where's the water coming from?"

He looked up at Peggy, knowing the answer at once.

"The river," they said together.

CHAPTER FIVE

Be Careful What You Wish For

When they reached the school, Peggy said goodbye and joined the girls. Tom joined the crowd of boys. The boys and girls filed into the school in two separate lines. They weren't supposed to talk, but today there was a buzz of whispers. Tom caught Peggy's eye as they entered their grade-three classroom. They weren't sitting long before the teacher made an announcement.

"The town has declared a state of emergency," she said. "The school is closing. You must all go home to help your families prepare for the flood."

"What about the dykes?" asked a girl.

"The dykes will slow the water for a while," said the teacher. "But they won't stop the flood."

Tom and Peggy met outside the school.

"Come on!" Peggy said, starting to run.

Tom joined her. He couldn't help grinning. He had gotten his wish for an extra day off school.

They climbed the first fence on their way home and stopped. The field had been damp when they walked through it earlier. Now, muddy water glistened on the surface. Green shoots of newly planted corn poked up through the water.

Sitting on top of the fence, Tom took off his shoes and socks and rolled up his pants. He jumped off the fence and landed with a splash. Peggy slipped off her shoes and socks and jumped.

They tried to hurry across the field, but the water came up to their knees in the low spots. Peggy had to hold up her dress. They crossed two more farms before nearing the fence around Tom's farm. Amos waited for them on the other side.

Tom was relieved to see his family's farm was still mostly dry. But the water was creeping under the fence,

filling ruts and holes. When Tom and Peggy climbed over the fence, Amos ran around behind them and barked excitedly. It was as if he was trying to herd them away from the rising water.

"Good boy, Amos," Tom said, reaching out to scratch the dog's head. "We're coming."

As they neared his house, Tom realized his second wish was coming true. But not in the way he had expected. He had wanted to go to the river to help. But now the river was coming to him.

CHAPTER SIX

Closing In

Peggy said goodbye and ran down the driveway toward her own house. Tom looked over his family's farm. No water had reached the house or barn yet. But he knew it was moving closer. The cows were usually at the far end of the pasture at this time of day. Today they stood close to the barn. A few cows mooed restlessly.

"I'm home!" Tom called as he entered the house. "They closed the school."

Tom's mom stood in the kitchen, holding a chair. She frowned for a moment, then sighed.

"I guess that's just as well," she said. "You can help move the furniture upstairs."

"Do you think the water will come into the house?" Tom asked.

"I hope not," said Mom. "But better safe than sorry."

Tom and Mom spent the next hour carrying furniture to the second floor of the house. Then they rolled up the living-room carpet and hauled it up the stairs. They dropped it in the hallway and sat down on top of it.

"I'm beat," said Tom.

"Me too," said Mom. She pushed a strand of damp hair off her forehead.

From the hallway, Tom could see through the open doors of the two bedrooms and the spare room. The rooms were crammed with furniture. He would have to climb over the kitchen table to get to his bed.

"Maaa! Maaa!"

"Moo!"

The calls of upset cows rose to the upstairs windows. Mom stood up.

"What's going on?" she asked. She and Tom hurried to a window.

Below, a large group of cows was gathered at the edge of the spreading water. In the middle of the water, on a small island of grass, stood a lone calf.

"Maaa!" the little calf cried.

"Moo!" answered its mother from across the barrier of water.

"We've got to rescue it!" said Tom.

CHAPTER SEVEN

Rescue

Tom and Mom hurried outside. While they had been busy moving furniture, brown murky water had crept up over the field around the cow barn. The cows were bunched in between the water and the barn. In front of the group stood one mother cow. Her head stretched out toward the calf who was stuck on the little mound of grass.

"Moo!" called the mother cow, as if calling the calf to come join her.

"Maa!" replied the frightened calf, refusing to budge.

Tom was still in bare feet. He rolled up his pants again and waded out to the calf's island. He stepped up behind her, set his hands on her hindquarters and pushed. The calf did not move.

"Come on," Tom said in a gentle voice. "The water's not deep. You'll be through it in no time."

The calf took one step into the water, then stepped back again. "Maa!"

Tom jumped out of the way before she could step on his feet. "It's no use," Tom called to Mom.

She stood beside the mother cow, her lips pursed together in thought.

"Stay right there a minute," she told Tom. She turned and disappeared into the barn and came out carrying a coil of rope. She tossed it across the water to Tom.

Tom looped the rope around the calf's neck and tied a knot. "Come on," he coaxed again, tugging on the length of rope.

The calf tried to keep her feet planted, but Tom pulled harder. The calf took one step into the water and mooed in distress. Tom held tight to the rope

as the calf tried to step backward again. He pulled
once more, and the calf took another step.

"That's it!" called Mom.

The calf stood with all four hooves in the water
now. It was only up to her knees, but she was still
frightened. The calf's mother and the other cows
mooed encouragement. Amos appeared from behind
the barn and ran up to join them. His barks added
to the noise.

"Maa!" cried the calf, looking at her mother.

Tom stepped forward, tugging on the rope. Suddenly the calf kicked up her hooves. She galloped the last few steps out of the water and onto dry land.

"Good work," Mom said to Tom. The calf nuzzled up beside her mother. Mom frowned. "They're all on dry land now," she said. "But not for long."

Tom and Mom looked at the muddy water that was creeping closer and closer to the barn and house.

CHAPTER EIGHT

Evacuation Plans

"Well," said Mom, "we won't be able to carry the cows upstairs like we did with the furniture."

Tom laughed, but he knew the problem was serious. He looked back at the little hill of grass on which the calf had been stranded.

"We need a big hill," he said. "Big enough to fit all the cows and all the people."

Mom nodded and looked thoughtful.

"Hello!" called a voice behind them. It was Peggy riding up the driveway on her bicycle. She stopped the bike and hopped off. Amos trotted over to sniff one of her legs, his tail wagging.

"I can't stay," Peggy said, keeping hold of her handlebars. "I've got to get back home to help pack. I just stopped by to tell you about the evacuation train. It's taking anyone who wants to leave to Vancouver."

"Are you going?" Tom asked.

"Just my mom, my little brother and me," Peggy told them. "My dad's still helping at the river. He and my older brothers are staying here with the cows."

Tom looked at Mom.

"What are we going to do?" he asked. A train ride to the city would be fun, but the Lone Ranger wouldn't evacuate. He would stay and help.

"I'd like you to be on that train," Mom said. "A flood is no place for children."

"But what about the cows?" said Tom. "There's no train for them."

"You're right," said Mom. "We'll have to figure out what to do with the cows. And we can't wait for your dad."

CHAPTER NINE

What to do?

"You could take them to the graveyard," Peggy said. She climbed back on her bike.

"The graveyard?" Tom and Mom said in surprise.

"My oldest brother, Jeff, is in charge of the cows while my dad is helping with the sandbags. Jeff says people are talking about moving all the dairy cows to the graveyard," Peggy said.

Mom pursed her lips. "It *is* the only big hill around," she said. "And there's enough clear space for the cows."

Peggy waved goodbye and pedaled off. "Good luck!" she called over her shoulder.

Tom watched Peggy go. He wondered what fun he would miss by staying here instead of going with Peggy on the train. But then he thought of the Lone Ranger again. The masked hero wouldn't leave on an evacuation train with a bunch of women and children. He would ride alongside on his noble horse, Silver, guarding the train from outlaws. And if there were no outlaws to worry about, he would stay behind and help with the flood—even if that meant taking care of cows.

Tom looked past Peggy to the steep mountain slopes rising in the distance. The river couldn't flood that high, but it would be impossible to get the cows up to the mountains. Down near the Fraser River, the ground was almost completely flat. If the river kept rising, it would spread out and cover all the farmland. If they didn't move the cows, the cows could drown.

There were very few high spots close by. The closest and largest one was the graveyard hill. It was covered with graves, but there was also grass.

"It could work," Tom said.

Mom nodded.

The problem was how to get the cows to the graveyard.

CHAPTER TEN

Tom's Plan

"We'll pack the pickup truck with supplies, and I'll drive it," Mom said. "The cows will have to walk, and you'll have to lead them."

Tom's eyes widened. "Lead them down the road?"

"There's no other way," said Mom.

As Tom and Mom loaded the truck with camping, cooking and milking supplies, Tom worried. How would he get the cows to walk down the road? And how would he get them to go where he wanted them to go?

He thought about the group of cows milling behind the mother cow as she called to her stranded calf. That mother cow was the leader. The other cows always followed her to the barn when it was time for milking. And she had followed her calf.

Tom smiled. He had an idea for how to move the cows.

When the truck was loaded and ready to go, Mom tacked a note for Dad to the back door.

Tom found the mother cow and her calf. Once more, he tied the rope around the calf's neck. He took hold of the loose end and gave a gentle tug.

"Maa!" cried the calf, resisting Tom's pull.

Tom held up a bundle of tender, sweet grass he had picked beside the driveway. The calf nosed the grass and opened her mouth. Before her teeth could get a good grip, Tom pulled the bundle out of her reach. The calf took a step after it. Tom walked forward, one hand holding the rope and the other holding the grass just out of the calf's reach.

The calf followed. Then the mother cow stepped forward, too, staying close to her calf.

Tom looked behind the mother cow. The other cows and the two other calves had stepped forward as well. They were following their lead cow. Tom grinned. His plan was going to work. There was just one problem. The graveyard was three miles west. He could walk with the cows for three miles, but he wouldn't be able to hold his arm out with a handful of grass for that long. He had to think of some other way to lure the calf forward.

CHAPTER ELEVEN

Amos Helps

Tom led the calf down the driveway, away from the barn and house. The cows followed. Behind them, Mom started up the pickup truck and began to slowly follow them. Amos barked happily as he trotted up to Tom's side.

Before they had reached the road at the end of the driveway, Tom's arm was already tired from holding out the grass. He put down his arm to rest it. The calf bumped her nose against his leg as she rooted for the grass. Tom yanked it out of her reach, taking a step sideways. The calf stepped after him, and all the cows behind her began to move to the side of the driveway.

"Keep them on the road!" called Mom out the window of the truck.

Amos barked from the middle of the driveway. It looked as if he was trying to get them back on track too.

"Okay, boy," Tom said. "We're coming." But inside, he did not feel so sure. He looked at the road ahead. How could he possibly keep the cows walking together for three miles?

Amos took a few steps and barked again.

"Hold on…" Tom started to tell Amos. But then he stopped. He looked at the brown leather collar around the dog's neck.

"Wait!" Tom told Amos. The dog sat obediently.

Tom caught up to Amos, pulling the calf along with him. Then he bent down and tucked the long blades of grass under Amos's collar.

"Okay, Amos," Tom said. "Lead the way!"

Amos barked and jumped to his feet. He seemed to know what Tom was saying. He began trotting ahead down the center of the driveway. The calf followed.

CHAPTER TWELVE

Cattle Drive

At the end of the driveway, Amos stopped and sat while Tom checked that no cars were coming. Tom pointed Amos to the left. Amos, Tom and the calf stepped onto the road and began walking. The whole herd of dairy cows followed. Behind them, Mom followed in the truck.

They were doing it! They were walking the cows down the middle of the road. It was like a parade—or better yet, it was like an old-fashioned cattle drive. And he and Amos were the Lone Ranger and Silver, leading the way. No cattle rustlers would get past them.

Tom wished Peggy was there to see him go by. But she had already left for the train. He continued down the road, walking proudly.

～

An hour later, Tom and the cows were still walking. Tom's legs felt heavy. It was getting harder and harder for him to lift one foot in front of the other. The cows were slowing down too. Tom wondered how much longer the lead calf and the others could last. They weren't used to this kind of walking. Also, it was getting late, and the adult cows would need to be milked soon.

They had covered a lot of ground. A few times they met a car coming toward them. Each time, the car had pulled off to the side of the road to let the cows pass. Tom had waved thanks to the drivers.

They soon met up with other dairy cows making their way to the graveyard. If Tom hadn't been so tired, he would have laughed at the strange sight they made.

As he walked, Tom wondered how his dad and the other men were doing on the dykes. And when would Dad be able to join them?

CHAPTER THIRTEEN

Tent City

Finally, they arrived at the graveyard. Tom led the cows up the hill to an empty patch of grass beside the rows of headstones. Mom drove the truck as far up the hill as she could, then parked.

Tom looked back down the hill toward the town and his family's farm. He could see the river in the distance, spreading past its normal banks. The water did not rush. It oozed and crept. The fields that he and Peggy had walked through that morning had been swallowed. Water licked around the houses. Ahead of the water, the road out of town was full of cows and vehicles making their way to the graveyard.

Tom left the cows grazing and headed down to help Mom unload the truck.

"We'll put the tent up over there," Mom said. She pointed at a spot where several canvas tents had already been set up. "We've got to get those cows milked and the milk trucked away before the road closes."

By the time all the work was done, the sun was beginning to set. Tom was exhausted. He slumped down on the ground beside their tent. Other tents had risen all around them. It was like a tent city full of bustling people.

"Here you go," said a woman whose hair was tied back with a yellow kerchief. She held out a cup of steaming coffee to Mom and one to Tom as well. Tom didn't really like coffee, but he took it gratefully.

"Thank you," Mom said with a tired smile. "It's been quite a day."

"Yes," said the woman with a tired smile of her own. "But with everyone working together, we'll get by."

Mom nodded and sipped her coffee.

"The Red Cross is feeding everyone tonight," the woman said. "So there's nothing to worry about."

That is good news, Tom thought. But as he looked down toward the dark, silent water, he wondered how his dad and the other men were doing on the dykes. This time, he did not wish he could be there with them.

CHAPTER FOURTEEN

Graveyard Island

When Tom woke in the morning, there were three people in the tent. Dad had joined them during the night. Mom was already up and opening the tent flap for Amos to go out. She saw Tom was awake and put a finger to her lips.

"Let him sleep," she whispered, nodding at Dad. "You and I can do the milking."

A few minutes later, Tom was standing outside the tent looking around. A patch of hill was covered with tents. A huge crowd of cows mooed and munched grass beside the gravestones. Tom looked down the hill and out toward the farms. Brown water seemed to cover everything. Branches, bushes and fence

51

posts floated on the surface. The roof of a chicken coop with a chicken still perched on it floated by. About the spot where the road used to be, someone was rowing a boat. The graveyard was now an island.

"Hey, Tom!"

Tom turned to see a boy waving at him from beside a tall headstone. It was Mike from his class at school.

"Do you want to play hide and seek?" Mike asked. Tom saw several other kids getting ready to hide among the gravestones.

"Sure!" Tom said. Then he remembered the cows. "After I help with milking," he added.

Partway through the milking, Dad joined Tom and Mom. He had not shaved since the start of the flood. His clothes were rumpled and dirty.

"I hear you were a big help yesterday," Dad said, resting a hand on Tom's shoulder. "I knew I could count on you."

Tom wanted to shrug off his dad's praise. He wanted to tell him it was all in a day's work for

the Lone Ranger. But he couldn't stop the smile that tugged at his mouth.

When the milking was finished, Dad put his hand on Tom's shoulder again.

"We might be here awhile," Dad said. "Some of the adults are meeting to make plans for getting the milk to market and supplies delivered. Do you want to join us?"

Tom felt a warm bloom of pride in his chest. Finally, he was getting included in the important stuff. He paused as he heard laughter and saw two kids running through the graveyard, dodging headstones.

"Home free!" one of them called.

Tom thought of the long walk with the cows yesterday and all the extra work he had done. Even the Lone Ranger needed a break sometimes. He looked up at Dad.

"Is it all right if I go and play?" he asked.

"Sure," Dad said with a grin. He ruffled Tom's hair with one big hand. "You've earned it."

CHAPTER FIFTEEN

Home

Tom and his parents stayed in the graveyard camp for almost three weeks. It took that long for the flood-water to finally sink and seep away.

When it was time to return home, Tom searched the graveyard for some long, tender shoots of grass that the cows hadn't already eaten. Dad laughed when Tom stuck the grass under Amos's collar and the cows started following Amos.

The walk home, however, was grim. Everything was covered with dark, stinking mud. The crops were ruined. Berry bushes and hop plants were dead. Dad said it would probably be awhile before they saw another rat or mouse.

Tom felt relieved when they herded the cows down their own driveway at last. He looked across the street to Peggy's house and wondered if she was back yet.

Tom and his parents had visited the farm the day before to assess the damage, repair fences and clean out the cow barn. Now, Tom opened the double gates to let the cows back into the field beside the barn. The sun was shining, and Dad said the ground would soon be dry.

"Let's have a break for lunch," Mom suggested.

The three of them stood looking at the house. Luckily the ground the house was built on was slightly higher than the rest of the farm. But a dark water stain skirted the bottom of the house. They had all looked inside yesterday and seen the mud that coated the rooms on the first floor. Now, Mom and Dad didn't seem to want to go back in.

"I don't know where we can eat," Mom said. She had packed them a lunch before leaving the

graveyard camp. It would be a while before the kitchen would be clean enough for the furniture to be moved back downstairs. She looked around the farm at all the mud.

"We could sit in the truck," Dad said.

Tom looked up at his bedroom window. The kitchen table was crowded into his bedroom with other pieces of furniture.

"Let's have a picnic inside," Tom said. "We could all sit on my bed."

Mom and Dad smiled.

"And later," Tom said, "we can find the radio and listen to the Lone Ranger."

Amos barked, as if in agreement.

Tom entered the house with his mom and dad. There was a lot of work ahead of them, but it was good to be home.

Jacqueline Pearce is the author of several books for children and young adults, including *Mystery of the Missing Luck,* also in the Orca Echoes series. Her stories are inspired by local history, nature and animals, as well as multicultural experiences. One of the things Jacqueline loves about writing is when the research leads her to interesting places, such as faraway Japan or the closer-to-home old Agassiz graveyard. Jacqueline grew up on Vancouver Island and currently lives in Burnaby, British Columbia, with her husband, daughter and two cats.

www.jacquelinepearce.ca